Flora's Family

A catalogue record for this book is available from
the British Library.

ISBN 978 1 84538 692 4

Written by Annette Aubrey
Edited by Sarah Medina
Designed by Alix Wood
Illustrated by Patrice Barton
Consultancy by David Hart

Publisher Steve Evans
Creative Director Zeta Davies
Senior Editor Hannah Ray

Printed and bound in China

Flora's Family

Annette Aubrey

Illustrated by
Patrice Barton

Flora was covered in bubbles,

Having fun in a lovely, warm bath!

Her mum and dad washed her and rinsed her
While she **shrieked** and she giggled and laughed.

4

And when Flora was all squeaky clean,
Mum dried her...

pat-a-pat, pat...

With the fluffiest,
big, yellow towel.

Then in front of the mirror they sat.

Mum used her own special hairbrush
To brush Flora's flowing, black hair.
Flora glanced into the mirror,
Then she stared
and she stared
and she stared.

Why's my hair so long and so dark, Mum,
When yours is so short and so fair?
And — look! — you have all of those freckles.
I can see lots of them, there, there and there!

7

"Let's sit with Dad," smiled her mother.
"We have something to share with you, see.
When you were a small, tiny baby,
You became part of our own family.

"You were a bouncy and bright-eyed baby
When we adopted you. It's very true!
We loved you, dear, from the beginning
And promised to take care of you."

Dad said, "Mum and I were delighted
To have another child to adore.
And your brother and sister were happy.
They couldn't have wanted for more.

"Now what would we do without you,
Our own funny Flora, so sweet?
You are the most delightful daughter.
With you, our family's complete."

"I don't understand it," said Flora.
"Daddy, what does it really mean
To be adopted? Am I very different?
Aren't I just like Jake and Eve?"

Mum kissed Flora and hugged her.
And Dad held both Flora's hands.
"Before the day that you were born,
Your birth parents made special plans."

14

And so they made a decision
That was hard and brave to do.
They chose to find a family
To **love** and to **cherish** you.

"But didn't they want to keep me?"
Said Flora to her dad.

"Did I do something awful?
Did they think that I was so bad?"

16

No, darling, that's not what happened.
They loved you — your birth mum and dad.
So much that they made a plan for you
To live the best life you could have.

17

"Your birth parents wanted to know
That you'd be loved and never alone.
And that's what all of us wanted
That day, when we brought you home.

"We're so happy now we're a family
And that we can love and can play,
And laugh at all of the funny things
That happen to us every day!"

"You're starting to have lots of questions,"
Said Mum. "Flora, that's very good.
Dad and I will answer them all
To make sure that you've understood.

"It doesn't matter how long it takes.
We have for ever and a day.

You can ask us a million times over
So that you know that you are okay."

Flora loved all of her family.
And she knew that they loved her, too.
"I may have dark hair, and yours is fair,
But I'm still a big part of you.

"You look after me and protect me
And you help me to learn and to grow."
Flora smiled, then giggled, then
laughed loudly.

"I'm the happiest girl that I know!"

23

NOTES FOR PARENTS AND TEACHERS

- Look at the front cover of the book together. Talk about the picture. Can your children guess what the book is going to be about?

- Turn to pages 4 and 5. Bathtime can be a fun family time. Talk about how much fun Flora is having with her mum and dad. Invite your children to talk about their bathtime fun.

- On page 7, Flora notices that her hair is long and dark, but that her mum's hair is short and fair. Ask your children if they had noticed that, too.

- On page 9, Flora's mum tells Flora that she has been adopted. Ask your children what they think it means to be adopted. Explain what adoption is, and answer any questions your children may have.

- Ask your children what they think Flora feels when she discovers she has been adopted. Do they know anyone who has been adopted?

- On page 10, Flora's mum and dad say how happy they are that Flora is part of their family. Ask your children how they think this makes Flora feel.

- On page 12, Flora asks if she is different from her brother and sister. Explain that adopted children are different in some ways (for example, they have different birth parents), but that they are the same in other ways (for example, they live in the same house, they have the same parents to look after them and they may like the same things). Ask your children to think about the ways in which Flora is different from the rest of her family, and the ways she is the same.

- On page 14, Flora's dad says that babies need a lot of care. Invite your children to talk about the kind of care a baby needs. Explain that all children feel safest and happiest when they know that their parents can look after all their needs. You could talk about this in terms of the parents being the 'big ones', who do the looking after, and the children being the 'little ones', who are looked after so that they can grow and learn. Emphasize that all children, including adopted children, are the 'little ones' in the family.

- On page 15, Flora's parents explain how hard it was for Flora's birth parents to decide to find an adoptive family for Flora. Discuss how this decision was made out of their love for her.

- On page 16, Flora worries that her birth parents did not keep her because she had done something wrong. This is a common concern for adopted children. Ask your children how they think Flora was feeling when she asked this question.

- On page 18, Flora's dad makes it clear that Flora's birth parents and her adoptive parents wanted to be sure that Flora felt loved and safe, and that she was taken care of. How do your children think Flora felt when she heard that?

- On page 20. Flora's mum says that it is good for Flora to ask lots of questions. It is important for adopted children to know that they can ask as many questions as they want. Explain that your children can ask questions, and that, like Flora's mum and dad, you will always answer them so they can understand.

- On page 22, it is clear that Flora's family love each other very much. Ask your children what they think it is that makes Flora happy. Talk about what they have heard in the story that would cause Flora to be so happy.